SCRIBBLES

BY: SAAKSHI TAILOR

Book*Squirrel* Publication

Book*Squirrel* Publication

Regd. Under MSME Act.

"SCRIBBLES"

By: Saakshi Tailor

ISBN: 978-93-89557-70-1

Language: English

1st Edition

Formatting: Muskan Shah

Cover: Ronak

AUTHOR'S NOTE

I am a student pursuing studies in class 12th Science Stream. I have been writing poems in class because of my lack of interest in science. Being out of the class, doing random things in the library, the food at my home, every silly single thing has always inspired me to write.

My parents have always supported me after they got to know about my writing skills. I was a bit demotivated when my Math and Physics faculties told me that, writing won't help you, come out from your imaginary world, they also called my parents, complained about my score and my writing habits between the class. Today I have written a book, a set of poems. I just want to say, I might have less interest in my subjects, but that really doesn't mean that people will disrespect the sentiments of a student and their interests.

I am just a common girl who found great interest in writing poetry. Writing wouldn't be possible for me if my parents, friends and teachers wouldn't have supported me.

Thanking everyone who encouraged me to write and come up with my book.

And a special thanks to every person who discouraged and tried demotivating me, just because of their words I am here completing a set of poems "SCRIBBLES".

ABOUT THE AUTHOR

Saakshi Tailor is a student of class 12 science. Daughter of Mr. Manish Tailor and Mrs. Hetal Tailor. Writing poems and reading is her hobby. She has motivational thoughts and does believe in motivating people around. She aims to write as much as she can to share her thoughts with the people around in every possible theme.

She believes writing is an art and writing has no fixed time or moods. Writing is a feeling that can be raised anywhere at any time. Thoughts are the most powerful weapon one can have. Her hobbies include scribbling and doodling which has the maximum inspiration over her writing. Reading and comparing imaginative fiction is one of her interests.

She believes in art and values art and literature in her life. Being from a Gujarati family, Saakshi can fluently speak Gujarati, she can also speak English and Hindi. She is fond of reading blogs and discover things over the internet.

THEME INDEX

THEME 1: SHADES OF LIFE

THEME 2: NATURE

THEME 3: STRAIGHT FROM THE HEART

THEME 4: MEMORIES

THEME 5: FOUR LINES AWAY

THEME 6: THE RANDOM WORLD

Theme 1

SHADES OF LIFE

Index

- Blue
- Dark
- Color to my life
- Canvas
- Fall

<u>BLUE</u>

Blue to my sky

Blue to my moon

Envy to thy

Envy to fly

Up to my sky

To the moon of the sly

To paint it in blue

Paint it too cool

Paint it at peace

Forever, ever and ever,

Painted to peace

Till the black shade of life comes to it

Oh!!! Glory to the power

Paint it blue

To burn the red

Red to my anger

Red to my tear

Paint it blue

To the due,

Ever thought to a blue world

The world being blue

Blue at peace

Blue at rest

Forever, ever and ever.

<u>DARK</u>

So dark like a bark

Is so impressive

The theme of dark

Looks so smark

The dark world

The dark light

The shades of dark

Even so far

Lock and the key

All dark

The life of worth

The shade of dusk

The dark winds

The firm hearts

Cozy nights

Dizzy days

All the dark souls

All in the deep sorrow

No grief no pain

All faints.

No visible tears

No counts

No notes

All go in the dark.

<u>COLOR TO MY LIFE</u>

Red to my love

To show it to my foe

Paint it red

To prove it bad

Green to my friendship

Beginning to ship

Yellow to my faith

Orange to my morning

Black to my mind

White to the soul

Just to be so pure

Too pure to be like a rainbow

Rainbow so beautiful

To the beauty of nature

Colors so beautiful

Never to be petty of sins

Enough colorful to color my mind

Color of my pain and despair

To the color of joy

Joy to my heart is

The only color I need to put in life.

<u>CANVAS</u>

No matter what you are

Someday there will be an artist

A perfectionist to prove u an art

People around likely to pun up

The art of life

Is a rule to fly

Wait for the time

The correct artist

Will me u a great part of an art.

<u>FALL</u>

Admiring the fall

The orange leaves come over

The brown woods

Coming of frosts

Down to the earthy land

I welcome the frost

To land up white.

Theme 2

<u>NATURE</u>

<u>Index</u>

- Ocean
- Dam of thoughts
- Bubble
- Big bang
- Bow
- Horizon
- Nature
- Letter to nature

<u>OCEAN</u>

Ocean of words

Ocean of nerds

So deep to explore

So much to see

Who knows what exists deep inside

The truth

The burn

The life

And the beginning

Till the death

The life below

The life above

Soo different to see

Not all we know what stays down

All we know the part of the world

Which say a lot about us

The life of us

Ancestry of us

All belong to the ocean of life.

Deep down there

The things go

My thoughts go

To see life

Thoughts take place

Make a world

The world of words

In the depth of deep down

The new beginning

All along with the new word

The new language

The new life

The new way

The way to grace

The way to express

To impress

A down inside

In my city of words

In the deep ocean.

<u>DAM OF THOUGHTS</u>

Dam of thoughts

Holds a lot

Tears of grief

Wishes to thee

Everything to flow

Splashes on the wall

The path to go

Soo much to fill

Soo much to add

Once full

The scene so beautiful

The flowing dam

The words of grief

The days of relief

All becomes calm once the

Dam of thoughts overflow life.

BUBBLE

Drowning deep inside

Just a blow to fly up high

Just a poke to burst the joy

Moving along the breeze so nice

The Bubble made my day so bright.

<u>BIG BANG</u>

A song so loud

For the world full of howl

Cowards of the world.

So much to know

So much to the almighty

All to the coward

Judge to the world

Who knows what to say

Who discovered what to know

A song so loud

No thoughts to go

New tunes to came

The thoughts to frown

Ready with the new crown,

The days are to a countdown.

<u>BOW</u>

Bow to the earth

Bow to the life

Bow to the creator

Surrender to nature

Acceptance to the fixture

Days of entity

To feel spry

To feel the strength

To feel the influence

Bow to the thy

In search of why.

<u>HORIZON</u>

The age of distinct views

I put upon my horizon

The never-ending war

Between the land and sky

The dusk the dawn

The clouds and the water

Ever buffering to meet

Seems quiet

But going on and on and on

To the never-ending illusion

The war continues

And the beauty illuminates

Over my horizon.

<u>NATURE</u>

The sound of life

The lights of fame

The fragrance of meadows

The glory of fall

The essence of taste

The rainy smells

The deep well

Horrifying oceans

Clear skies

The rear rainbows

The windy collars

The dizzy moon

High noon

The gloomy lands

Tasty bands

Creamy life

Bright lights

High dreams

Soo much to see

Soo much to learn

Nature slays always with fun.

LETTER TO NATURE

The letter to nature

Unposted in the heart

Just the memories

The flowing brook

The calming boats

The pretty sunsets

The fresh dawn

The first drops of rain

And the earthy fragrance

Blooming flora

The blue sky

The rainbow sight

The only reason to make a sight

Wandering ever around the unposted letter to the love nature.

Theme 3

STRAIGHT FROM THE HEART

Index

- A day without you
- Be you
- Courage
- Blink
- Charm
- Isn't it great
- Tears to your pillow never lied
- The day you changed
- Untold pages
- Quick
- United

<u>A DAY WITHOUT YOU</u>

I imagine the day

Turning to a ray

The day I met you

To the day

I spent without you

The days spent so well

To the days spent alone

All I needed was you

To be a permanent flue

To make my life so true

The fortune to my book

A slay at my look

All worthless on a day without you

Looking at them

Giggling over then

Was a blank canvas on a

Day without you

The shitty talks

The stupid walks

Lay them all

To the wall of fate

To the hope that never dies

To the loop that never ends

A day without you

Seems long to end

The endless walks

The sleepless talks

Crying together

Being silly forever, all is just with you.

<u>BE YOU</u>

Ever thought of being empty bored

Look up wake up shake-up

Let the little chill in you roll out

Ever wondered of not speaking out

Look at the frame

The burning flame

In the wane

Let it let your flame

Speak up out of your wane

If not

Then the flame will blow

Put you down to sorrow

Deep down you will know

It was my day for so

But the day you wake up

Chill up and scream up

You will find your world

Burnt in the jealously of your flame.

COURAGE

A little book

Soo many pages

Soo many chapters

All to a way of laughter

Way to sorrow of emotions

One book never to be part

Never enough to describe the circle of life

Every stanza makes a new day

Every page makes a new year

Though it will never show up on my world to the thy

Ever thought the world so high

Or maybe me being too low

A bucket of courage to tell the world

I'm the only one to rule my words.

<u>BLINK</u>

Tonight to the fairytale

A story of a little bird

Ever heard about a bird in a cage

Alone in the world

Nobody to listen

Just a blink and world is your

A wink of words

Extreme loud

Enough to get a huge crowd

Every single dying to word out

A blink of courage to step up

Courage to speak up

The mind full of thoughts

Creating a projection

Buckle up your life

Pack up your stuff honey

The world is waiting

The jury of life is waiting

The reward to be given

The award to be taken

All just in a blink

The world under your step

The world will wake you up

Just a headline

Will make your world shine

Just wake up blink

And the world is your just in a wink

Wanna try a game of world

Come join me

Just a blink and enter a dream

Step up buck up

The world is waiting.

<u>CHARM</u>

Burying down a little charm

In hope for a little on to die

But didn't know

The little was a seed

Watered buy rain inspired by darkness

Brought up sun

Buried into the nature's lap

Peacefully making no noise

Grows out making a whole new world

Coming up over the expectancies

Mother nature's nurture

the love of air

Nourished by the clouds

Grows the beauty,

The beauty of carefully nurtured charm.

ISN'T IT GREAT

The days to cherish

Comes back to me, I wish

They holiday in

Back to win

They cherish thee up to ring

The bell at the door

The well at the forth

Water in the flow

And being high to a flaw

Isn't it great?

To get it back

Carry a bag pack

Moving around in thee

The Beauty of the sin

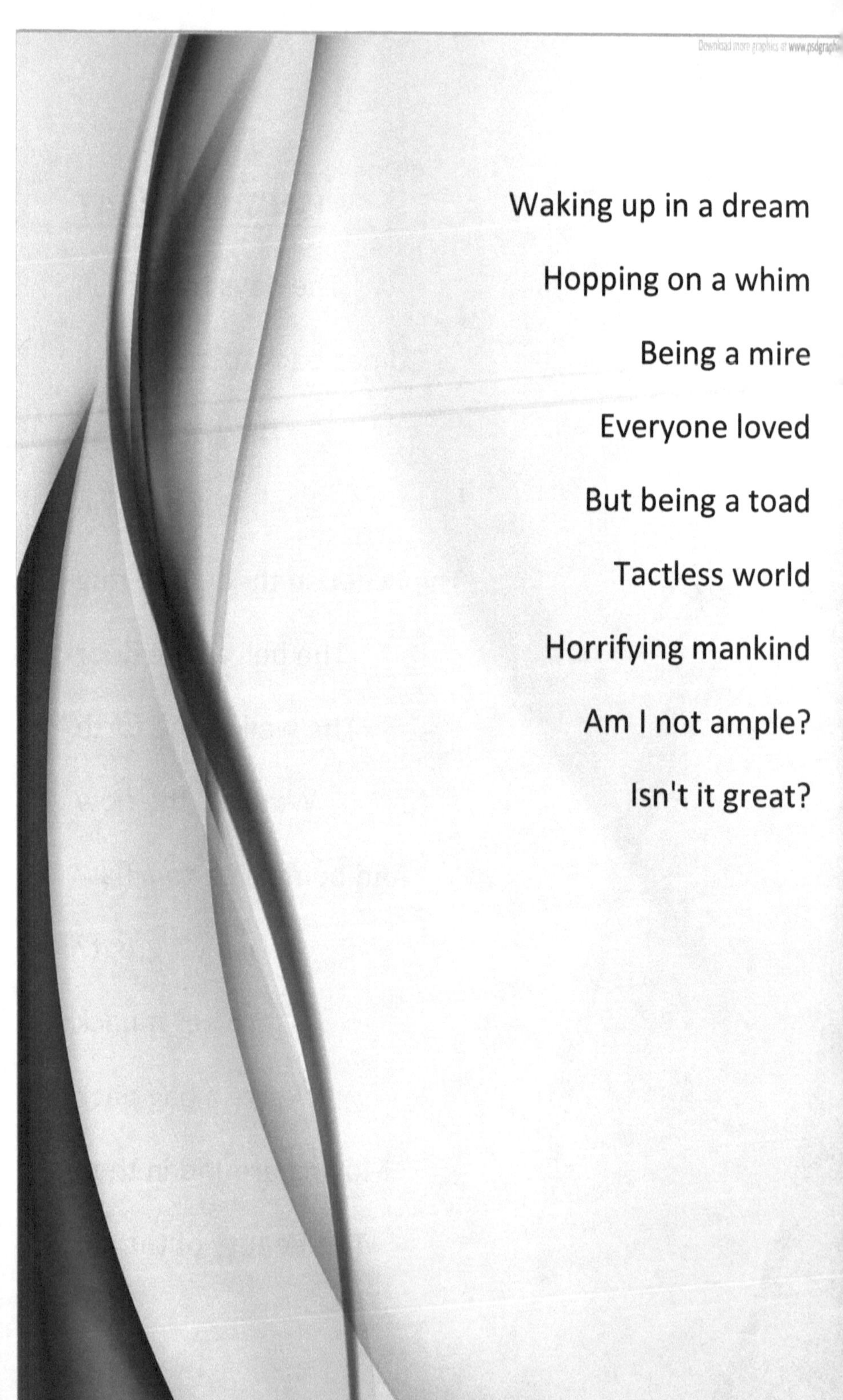

Waking up in a dream

Hopping on a whim

Being a mire

Everyone loved

But being a toad

Tactless world

Horrifying mankind

Am I not ample?

Isn't it great?

<u>TEARS ON YOUR PILLOW NEVER LIED</u>

The day you cried for no reason

Maybe the acceptance of the god's prison

The day you cried for your self

Will be the day you create your self

The tears to your pillow

That raises you to high from low

The day you cried to your pillow

The day you spent for joy

The tears you lost for sorrow

The truth to the pillow

Dream to your bed

The pillow knows it's all dead

The day comes alive

The tears of sorrow turn to the life

The only tears of joy

Comes back like a toy

A toy of glass to be taken care of

Once broke may tear you off

The tears to your pillow never lied.

THE DAY YOU CHANGED

The day you changed for me

The way you changed to be

The way you left me

The way you taught thee

The World around too big for you

The world you live in too bijou

The way I spent days talking around

The way it felt while I saw u stalking around

The world to small to sit it

The room to huge to stay in

The corner greatest to test me

The patience of my mind

And the beginning of my world

All begins today

Set to devote me to the creator

Choose the creator as a mentor

The day to took away my world

The way my mentor teaches to live the world

The day you took away my joy

The way my mentor teaches to glee

The day you changed

The day I lived the world.

THE UNTOLD PAGES

The untold pages

The horrified scribbles

With zeros on the papers

Holding me so tight

Even a paper can't move my sight

The untold pages of my life

The only thing that fights

The unread pages

The incomplete stories

All die together in an untold page of mine.

<u>QUICK</u>

So quick to see

But no to hear

So quick to judge

But not so witness

Moving so swift

We miss the world

The foe of life is taken together

With the fro

And the friend is judged out the light

Being so silly

Do we be happy?

Moving so fast

Leaving the time

Everything so fine

Moving back on nine

The time goes fast

The days come slow

Live the moment or let it flow

That's all we need to know.

<u>UNITED</u>

Religious speak

Truth neat

Every possible way

Kept allowed to speak aloud

Thousand languages

United to country

So many pieces of virtually

Put together in a single nationality

Hard to believe into reality

Holding the autonomy

Tons of thoughts

In trillions of people

Holding the immortal heritage

Rich of culture

And millions of costumes

Filled with zeal

Just like a jigsaw

Put together

The way was someday better.

Theme 4

MEMORIES

Index

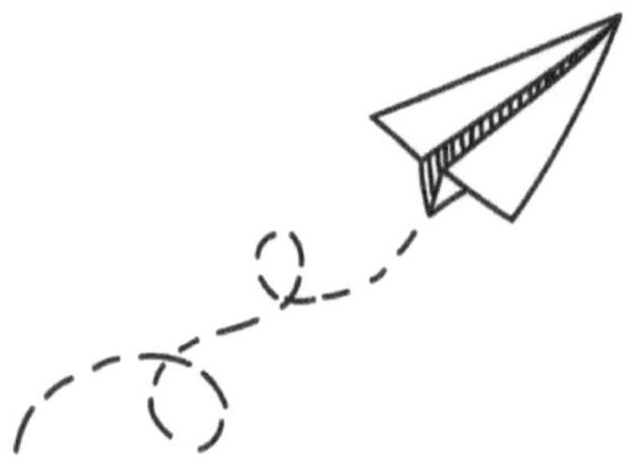

ESSENCE

The window of memories

The source of memorials

The doors of your cupboard

And the wind chime on the window

The pure flavor of life

With the heartfelt essence of love

The essence of purity

The essence of you spread over the view

The view from the window of memories

The chimes on the window

Tell the story

The stories of your life

Adding fragrance to the essence

Making it is the, Perfect essence of life.

DECK OF CARDS

You never know what comes next

Still, we always want to think what comes next

Just like a game of card

Who knows who plays the card out

But still, we play upon

The story of luck

Going on for years

The arranged deck of cards

Who knows what's next

But still playing on is confidence

And moving on and on is the experience

Life goes on to the next game

Even if you loose

A new game of shuffled deck

A new chance of coming up back.

<u>FLASH</u>

Flash of light

Splash of water

The sounds of the well

The sounds of the bell

All I remember is the flashbacks of my life

Playing in the park

Dreaming the dark

The days of joy to

The plays of life

The characters so good

From being too shy

To being too sly

The days to the flashback

The days that never be back

The numbing waters off well

To the bright mornings of the dell

Those numb mornings

Those cozy blankets

The only flash I remember

Deep inside still searching

News flash

New story

The same innocent glory.

TOWN AROUND

Town so nice,

Town so bright

The city of light is so bright.

Moving along with roads of joy

The crossing of rainbows

To the noble bows

The noble deans move towards the dream

The dream of life, on away,

The dream of glory, on a Flory day,

Down to my Town Tonight,

On the way to the worldly carvings

Down to my town, Town of colors, Town of joy,

Come up once, to make a ray

The days of joy, To the town so nice.

<u>DREAM</u>

When you dream to do

When you be to fro

But life tells you

How papers crumble dream

A creamy dream

Garbage into stream

Stream to the ocean

And ocean to the sky

Back to the earth

Being so usual shy

Dream tonight leaves a fright

To live the world

To feel the world but

Hence to know that

Dream to do is

The goal to do

Every time with a flow to go

The path to choose

Eyes to close

The way to glory

And a dreamy story

Begins with the daydream

Releases a sword

A sword of words to

Fight the world

A thunder of the lightning storm

The storm of words

The storm of dream

The storm of the day with the dream

All together to make

A dream come alive

In a stormy day

Making life alive

And telling the truth to almighty

That

Life is but a dream.

MEMORIES

So much to see

Soo much to miss

But something that is always quizzed

Ever wondered the past

The love of life

In the lap of time

Every moment so precious to see

Birth of a body

To the vision of the child

Coming of the youth

And going off to school

All in a box of wishes

To get back the quickies

Soo much to do

Too much to fro

But hence stays ever in the box of dear

The beginning of life

Live in a home

Being alone

Or in a lane

Every moment so deep to find

Back to the line

Every time I see the box of mine

Filled with memories so fine.

Theme 5

FOUR LINES IN A WAY

Index

- Why??
- A Day
- Star
- Daydream
- War
- Picture
- Nightmare

<u>WHY??</u>

Why does the horizon meet?

Why do the thoughts greet?

Why is the world so sweet?

Even after having a bad week.

<u>A DAY</u>

Days of beauty

Days of glory

All cherish

In the day of the story.

<u>STAR</u>

Star light, Star bright

May you know deep down tonight

That everything will be alright

That's my only wish tonight.

<u>DAYDREAM</u>

Good day, food day

Being happy all-day

Shiny morning, bright day

The only wish that happens today

Have a nice day.

<u>WAR</u>

All in a word

Foul in the surd

Coming back to the game

With a sword of nerd.

<u>PICTURE</u>

So calm, so still

But can move a body apart,

dividing the thoughts

Reminding the flaws, just a piece of paper

This memorizes a whole lot.

NIGHTMARE

Someday, Dark day

The day of sorrow

The day of the morrow

That never comes over the morrow.

Theme 6

THE RANDOM WORLD

Index

ALGORITHM

Fun to life

Every day everyone enjoying

Eager to solve the algorithm of life

Once solved

The new day comes with a new algorithm

If not then believe and make a new try to prove up the

Previous one

And if the day won't appear its algorithm

Believe in you

And make your theorem to solve the most difficult

Algorithm ever coming to you the next morrow.

<u>NO</u>

Never to the malign

Acceptance to the wicked world

Corrupt to the self-doubt to the deep

All you know is

The jury of life decides

Whether to live or die.

<u>WALL OF DREAMS</u>

Its midnight an innocent staring at the wall

Who knew that the wall stood tall

It stood tall to the dream come alive

It stood tall to failure to die

The day I grew up staring the wall

Creating a view off all

All my dreams come alive tonight

The star that shines so bright

Brings me my present so right

The beauty of the wall changes every night

Wall changes its colors every night

The dream of color and joy

Changes the wall that stood tall

It shows me the endless vista

The rising of the moon to

The shedding off noon

The wall of the dream comes alive

Nature comes alive tonight

To meet me at my sight

At the same wall of dreams tonight.

LOOP

To the infinite memories

Live in a loop of diaries

All on a plan of being alive

Moving around on the alley

On this phase of life

In this path on a loop

All on away

To a destination at a bay

Lovely sands earthy greens

All to be captured in a loop of memories

On the alley of life.

<u>RANDOM</u>

Thoughts and sighs

To the dream so high

Moving around where no one knows

Being random when everyone bows

The critter of the time

The fly of the sky

Have no thoughts of being so.

Why?

Ever the clouds of nine

Moves random being so fine

Ever the river flowing so fine

Flows down being so chime

The questions of times

Flows with mind

Mind of thought

Questions so fought

All for a random piece of me.

<u>THE</u>

So good to say

But not to do

Always included

Never excluded

Completes the line

Respects the word

Most important

Word of line

Making sentence

Irony of life.

<u>NUMBER</u>

The Number on the desk

The date on the mat

Counting back the days

Counting the words

Numbers on the wall

The frame of the wall

Counting the cost

Counting the day

The day to come

The day to go

The number goes on till life

Numbers on calendar

Numbers on notes

Number of contacts

Numbers to a special day

All will be on time

Keep counting till the line.

LIFE`S VIBE

The day of victory

The day of the story

In the way of life

The play so nice

All together to prove

A light feather

The calm waters

The flourished brooks

Waiting for all the time

To flow up and get shook.

PATTERN

Pattern to the world

The world of lines

The days of nine...

Everything was just too fine

What happened when it became mine

The patterns of mind

The line to the world

Highlight the work

My work to my world

My space of pattern

My jar of light

Bars to my brain

Curves to my life

Stay it to life, Till the end of my thy.

<u>THE THRONE</u>

The power of joy

The power of nature

All into a crown

The silvery of words

The sighs of culture

All removed by the crown of joy

The joy of urbane

So high to form a crust

The day of rupture

Not to away from a huge beautiful culture

The beauty of the throne

To the luxury of the day

All in the crown to the city of a frown.

<u>SCRIBBLES</u>

The journey of me

Picking upon thy

To the creator

Woke up by a noise

The scribble on the wall

The scribble inspired to write upon

The journey took a turn

From the meaningless lines

To the sonnets so fine

The scribble on the wall

To the sheet of paper

Needed a lot of pamper

The scribble pampered became the inspiration

And the nurture on the sheet

Brought up the verse

The verse of my life

Just cause of the scribble on the bailey.

THE MUSICAL NOTE

In the world of sounds

I made my note

The note of my silvery life

The tones off my life

A new vibration to the world of my silvery strings

The tinkling fillies

Calling a new beginning

A new phase to my silvery notes

Added a new joy to the life

I don't know whether it's high

Or maybe a low

All I need to know is

To set my silvery

All just to the silvery note.

<u>TODAY</u>

 Dust in the sky

Clear to the ambition

Waiting for the dusk

To give up a flaw

Beginning back in the air

With a good new dawn.

MYSTERY

Who knew what was done

Who did what needed to be done

Waiting for a disclosure

And a letter to the order

Lying down over the area

Questions aroused

All over the fouls

The locked room

And a truth groom

Come together to give up and mystery forever.